MR TIGER,
BETSY
and the
GOLDEN
SEAHORSE

MR TIGER, BETSY and the GOLDEN SEAHORSE

Sally Gardner

illustrated by
Nick Maland

ZEPHYR
An imprint of Head of Zeus

9 7 5 3 1 2 4 6 8

A catalogue record for this book is available from the British Library

ISBN (HB): 9781788546614
ISBN (E): 9781788546607

Typesetting & design by Jessie Price

Printed and bound in by Spain by Unigraf S.L.

Head of Zeus Ltd
First Floor East, 5–8 Hardwick Street, London EC1R 4RG
www.headofzeus.com

To Meg, with all my love.
— SG

To Sally, Mark, Felix, Mabel
and Hector, with love.
— NM

·◆ 1 ◆·

We, the alphabet, are a family of letters. It is, we agree, a rather large family. Nevertheless, we muddle along without too many hiccups. We see ourselves as magicians of words. We sprinkle spells, make up stories, tell tall tales, spin yarns into a fabric of fables.

We come from an island that has been left off the map of the world.

This is where we first met Mr Tiger

a blue moon ago. We asked him if he would like to be the author of these books and we also asked Betsy K Glory. Both said no, they were far too busy having adventures. Mr Tiger gave us one of his speeches. He is fond of speeches and he said that we were more than capable of writing the tales of Mr Tiger and Betsy in our own way.

So, we washed our faces, tied our shoelaces, put on our Sunday best and now, with once upon a times and a bag full of happy endings, we are ready. Let's begin at the beginning.

·←· 2 ·→·

etsy **K Glory** lives with her dad, Alfonso Glory, as we're sure you know by now. He is the best ice cream maker on or off the map of the world. They live together in a tall windy house on the harbour. Downstairs is Dad's café and kitchen, and upstairs is their flat. From there they can look out of the windows on to the busy quayside below where the boats bob up and down in the blue sea.

Betsy has bright purple hair, shiny green eyes and the sweetest freckly face. Her mum, Myrtle, is a mermaid, and as feet and mermaids' tails don't mix, Mum lives mostly in the sea. Dad and Betsy, who both have feet, live mostly on the land, but Myrtle knitted Betsy a mermaid suit so she could swim and breathe underwater. So, all is as wonderful as Wednesday with Betsy K Glory.

Next, we must introduce Mr Tiger and his Gongalong acrobats.

A drum roll, please.

Mr Tiger wears a long buttoned-up tiger coat, a top hat and smart pointed shoes. He has a magical pocket-watch, which is very useful in adventures, and a compass so he never gets lost. But most amazing of all he has a circus of acrobats, is the captain of a blue-and-white-striped ship and recently has had a submarine built to his own design. His troupe of acrobats come from Gongalong Island that

is ruled by Princess Albee, a good friend to Betsy and Mr Tiger. The Gongalongs are less than a quarter of the size of an average human being, as delicate as china cups and as strong as cement. The acrobats also happen to be rather bouncy and have no fear of heights. This is just as well because it took a very tall ladder for them to climb to the moon where they put on a circus show that was out of this world.

Now, on with the story.

·← 3 →·

After Mr Tiger and Betsy's last adventure, when the baby sea dragon was saved from pirates and the islanders were rewarded with golden apples, Princess Albee and the mayor had announced they would send builders to make the Glorys' tall windy house a more mermaid-friendly home for Mum. The mayor had declared the work would start 'tomorrow'. But as is the way with

tomorrows, they tend to get lost in today. Princess Albee and her fiancé, Septimus Plank, the pastry chef, had sailed back to Gongalong Island to prepare for their wedding. They were followed by Mr Tiger's ship, because the acrobats too had to go home. Without the right kind of diet, only to be found on Gongalong Island, they would lose their bounce and without their bounce — well, they wouldn't be acrobats.

After they'd sailed away, the mayor had looked at the town's pennies and thought that he might have been a little rash in thinking the town could afford the work the house required. Especially after the expense of the Festival of the Sea Dragon.

Everything was further delayed by Princess Albee's wedding. It was to take place in a month's time and Dad had been asked to make the filling for Septimus's ice cream wedding cake.

Dad was worried. Dad was often worried, but this time he had good reason. How could he make the ice cream if there were builders in his kitchen? In short, and to make a blunt point as sharp as a 2B pencil, he decided that the building work should wait. Wedding cakes are very important, and cement and ice cream don't mix. Not to mention the upheaval, the cost ... and where would he and Betsy live while it was going on?

'I can go and live with Mum,' said Betsy. 'Remember, I have my mermaid suit — and I would love to see Mum's home.'

Dad agreed that even if the building work wasn't done this side of never, Betsy should go and stay with her mum. After all, there were many members of Mum's family that she hadn't yet met. And that is just what Betsy did.

Two weeks later on a Tuesday,
Mr Tiger's new blue-and-white
striped submarine bobbed up in

the harbour. A crowd gathered to greet him and ask when the circus would be coming back.

'My dear ladies and gentlemen, I thank you for your welcome. The circus...'

The crowd cheered.

'...the circus will be back soon to soonish,' said Mr Tiger as he made his way up the harbour steps. 'This is only a short visit. I am here to collect Betsy K Glory.'

'But she's not here,' said Dad, coming to meet him. 'She's gone to stay with Myrtle.'

Mr Tiger put a paw on Dad's shoulder. 'Then we have a slight problem, Alfonso. The wedding of Princess Albee to Septimus Plank has been brought forward.'

They went into the café.

'Why,' said Mr Tiger, 'it's the same as it's always been. Where are the water slides, the water lifts, the water beds?'

'The mayor said there wasn't enough money — and I have to say, I can't afford to stop work.'

'No, this will not do,' said Mr Tiger. 'It will not do at all. I will speak to Princess Albee and the mayor. People shouldn't give their word and then just take it away.'

We, the letters of the alphabet, agree. Too often we find ourselves used in the wrong way. But that's another story.

'Oh dear, please don't bother,' said Dad. 'You see, I'm not sure about it. How could I run my café with all the building work?

'Think of the mess,
The dust and the dirt,
Of all the stress,
Not to mention the plaster.
Making ice cream
Would be a disaster.'

'Now is not the time for doubt,' interrupted Mr Tiger. 'Doubt only makes a hole in a perfectly good decision. While the building work is taking place, you, my dear Alfonso, are going to live on my ship, which is on its way back to harbour.'

'Really, I don't think...'

'How is the ice cream for the wedding cake coming along?' asked Mr Tiger.

'Nearly done,' said Dad with his fingers crossed behind his back.

'Good. That's why I'm here. Princess

Albee has invited the moon and a few of the stars to be guests of honour at her wedding. The moon replied, saying it could only be there when it was full, so the wedding is to take place a week tomorrow, on Wednesday. As Betsy is the only bridesmaid, she is needed on Gongalong Island, pronto.'

Which means straightaway.

'It's all very rushed, but at least it doesn't involve an adventure,' said Dad. Then he saw Mr Tiger take out his pocket-watch and study the picture on it. 'Or does it?'

'Tigers have their secrets and their whiskers,' said Mr Tiger, 'their tales and their tails. You are right, Alfonso. An adventure is indeed calling.'

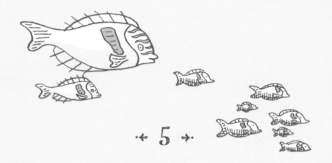

Myrtle Glory, tell us your story,
How does your garden grow?
With cockle shells and shipwrecked
bells
And anemones all in a row.

Deep, deep down under the blue, blue sea, where the sunshine keeps its spare rays of light, Betsy's mum lived in a beautiful pink shell house at the tail end of Mermaid City. From the outside it looked higgledy-piggledy and on the

inside it was as neat as a captain's whistle. At the back of the house was a sea garden with sea grass, cockleshell paths and sea anemones growing in a rockery. Betsy had never seen so many brightly coloured plants: mushrooms of different sizes in purples and pinks, grasses with bright yellow tips that wiggled and lit up, tall corals glittering with rainbows.

In the middle of Mum's garden was a statue that once had been the figurehead of a ship.

'I knew you would have a beautiful house and garden,' said Betsy when she first saw where her mum lived. 'I just knew.'

Everything Mum owned was made out of driftwood or things she'd found at the bottom of the sea. Her plates came from a fifteenth-century Spanish shipwreck, her goblets were the finest sparkling glass. Betsy had her own bedroom. Her bed had once been a rowing boat and the curtains were made from fishermen's nets.

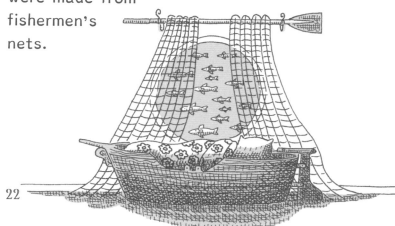

For the past
two weeks, Betsy's life
had been a whirlpool of visits
to Mum's friends and family,
meeting her nephews and nieces,
eating shrimp teas and fish suppers.
And today they were going to visit
the sea pig, who lived in an ancient
shipwreck that had been blown off
the map of the world along with the
sea pig.

'What's a sea pig?' asked Betsy.
They were eating breakfast in the
garden. Sunlight beamed through
the water and passing clouds of fish
swam above them.

'Once,' said Mum, 'when the world
was brand new to man and man was
brand new to the world, people
believed monsters and dragons

lived in the
oceans. They
made a map with
drawings showing all
the beasts — such as a huge octopus
with vast tentacles that had the
strength to capsize a ship. And an
enormous sea pig.'

'Well, they
were right about
the sea dragon,'
said Betsy,
thinking of the Pap-a-naggy and his
wife, the Mam-a-naggy, who lived in
a sea orchard somewhere down there.

'Surprisingly,' said Mum, 'they
were right about everything, though
they didn't know it. When they didn't
find any monsters,
they thought they

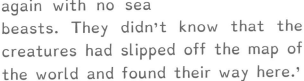

must be wrong
and drew the map
again with no sea
beasts. They didn't know that the
creatures had slipped off the map of
the world and found their way here.'

'Crumble cakes,' said Betsy.
'That's a bit worrying. I mean, an
enormous octopus...'

Mum sighed. 'You're right. The
octopus is a cantankerous old thing.'

'What does cantankerous mean?'
asked Betsy.

'Bad-tempered, crusty and grumpy.'

'And he's down here?'

'Yes,' said Mum. 'He is, at the
moment, living in the mouth of
the treasure seekers' cave.'

'Why?'

'Because he

thinks he's guarding lost treasure.'

'Lost treasure?' said Betsy. Things were getting better and better. 'Perhaps he'll show it to me.'

'Oh, no,' said Mum. 'The octopus doesn't let anyone near the cave.'

'That's a pity,' said Betsy. 'What about the sea pig?'

'The sea pig...?' said Mum absent-mindedly. 'Oh, yes, thank you. I nearly forgot.' And she took a large shell from a shelf in the kitchen.

'Ready?' she said, planting a kiss on Betsy's head. 'Are you wearing your seahorse necklace?'

'I haven't taken it off since Princess Albee gave it to me,' said Betsy.

Closing the garden gate behind them they swam off through the

coral forest, past rows of mermaid houses, out on to the rolling sandy seabed. And there it was, the most spectacular galleon, its tattered sails moving with the waves.

'Wow,' said Betsy.

'The sea pig is very proud of it,' said Mum.

'Look,' said Betsy, pointing. 'Seahorses. They're so beautiful and there are —' she counted — 'twelve of them.'

'Twelve? Then it's true,' said Mum.

'What's true?' asked Betsy.

'Pudding Pie is missing.'

'What is Pudding Pie?' asked Betsy, baffled. Life under the sea was so different to life on land. On land she understood what things meant, here so much was a watery mystery.

'Pudding Pie,' said Mum, 'is the most famous racing seahorse there has ever been. No seahorse has won more races or is more valuable. But I read in the *Tide Times* that Pudding Pie has vanished. The sea pig owns her and is most upset.'

Betsy's green eyes shone.

'A mystery!' she said. 'You know who we need...'

'Mr Tiger,' said Mum.

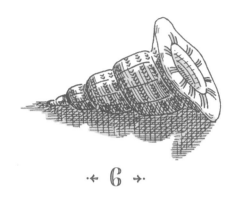

·← 6 →·

Mum always took with her a
large shell when she visited
the sea pig. Without it she
would never have understood what
the sea pig had to say, and he
wouldn't have understood her. He
made a sound that was like a honk
and at the same time wasn't like a
honk at all. And he honked as fast
as two horses galloping in different
directions.

Much the same could be said for

the way he looked: he wasn't like a pig and he wasn't unlike a pig. He had scales all over his body, webbed feet and a curly fishtail. Tufts of fur stood up along his back. Betsy would never have said so but she thought he was the ugliest creature she had ever seen. She stayed quietly next to Mum, listening.

The sea pig's speech sounded ghastly, full of bangs and wriggles, letter boxes and hand claps.

Mum had put the shell to her ear.

'What's he saying?' asked Betsy.

Mum translated, speaking into the shell. 'He said, "Myrtle! I weep! I cry! I'm wrecked on the rocks of ruin — Pudding Pie has been stolen!"'

'Not wrecked, dashed,' honked the sea pig. He stopped, wiped his eyes with a spotted hanky, then said, 'Who is this small, you-like thing with freckles?'

'My daughter, Betsy,' said Mum into the shell.

The sea pig held out a very clean webbed foot to Betsy.

'I am — or I would be — enchanted to meet you if I wasn't so miserable.'

He dabbed his eyes.

As we're underwater, thought Betsy, *it's hard to see if he's crying or not. He does have red eyes, but there again he's a sea pig and perhaps that's normal.*

'You'd better come in,' said the sea pig. 'I hate to think what has happened to Pudding Pie, though I think it's that cantankerous octopus who has taken her.'

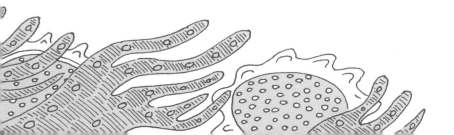

Betsy, of course, couldn't understand a word, but she followed him and Mum. Inside, the galleon was like an underwater museum with framed watercolours, a cannon and a treasure chest. They went down a staircase to the sea pig's living quarters, which were rather grand. The sea pig flapped on to an armchair. Betsy and Mum swam to a rainbow-coloured sofa. Around the cabin were rosettes, silver cups and pictures of the sea pig with Pudding Pie.

'Tell me what happened,' said Myrtle into the shell.

Betsy had almost given up listening when she noticed a beautiful silver teapot on the table in front of her. She was wondering what had happened to its lid, when to her

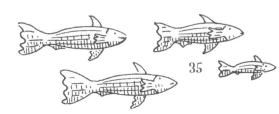

surprise a seahorse popped out and swam towards her.

'She's so pretty,' said Betsy. 'What's her name?'

Just then she thought she felt her

necklace tingle. Puzzled, she put her hand to it.

'Oh, her,' honked the sea pig.

Mum translated. '"She's called Silly Sausage and I tried to train her for racing but she's hopeless — useless over the sticks. And she's too small. But I love the silver teapot and she comes with it."'

What Betsy thought was that Silly Sausage looked miserable. Something was wrong, but Betsy was wise enough to say nothing.

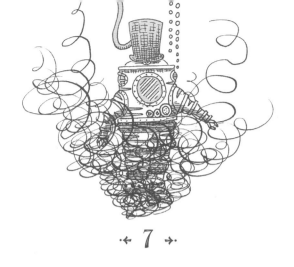

·← 7 →·

Betsy was in the garden, studying Mum's old map of the oceans, when a passing jellyfish made her look up. Beyond the garden gate, she could just make out a creature clanking towards her. It was hard to see because its feet disturbed the sandy seabed and the sand partly hid it from sight. What she could see was truly alarming. It was huge and made out of metal. Bubbles were coming from a tube at its back. It had metal gum boots and massive metal arms that ended in grappling claws. One of these was waving at her in a not altogether friendly-looking way.

Betsy was too frightened to wait any longer and wisely swam indoors.

'MUM!' she cried. 'There is a METAL MONSTER in the garden.'

Mum, who was making seaweed soup, looked out of the kitchen window as the garden gate swung open.

'Well, who would've thought?' she said. 'If it isn't Mr Tiger in a diving suit.'

Betsy looked too, and now she could see Mr Tiger's face and whiskers behind the glass front of the

metal helmet. And on top of the helmet perched Mr

Tiger's unmistakable top hat with all its many safety features.

'Where did you get the diving suit and how come you are here? I've really missed you, Mr Tiger,' said Betsy.

Mr Tiger took clumsy steps, and slowly, with a little help from Betsy, he made his way into the kitchen and sat down.

It was hard to hear what he was saying through the helmet until he adjusted the volume, which took some time.

At last he said, 'Water is not my natural habitat, but with this amazing suit and my brand-new submarine, not to mention my pocket-watch, I was able to find you both quite easily.'

'Dear Mr Tiger,' said Myrtle, 'you've gone to so much trouble to be here. I can't thank you enough.

Is the situation as bad as rumours suggest?'

Mr Tiger said something that Betsy thought was, 'Perhaps pigs might fly,' but he was talking about Pudding Pie.

After a few more misunderstandings, Mr Tiger said, 'I wonder, Myrtle, if I might borrow Betsy. I would like to take her and show her my new submarine. I can talk to her there without wearing this diving suit.'

Betsy's tail tingled with excitement.

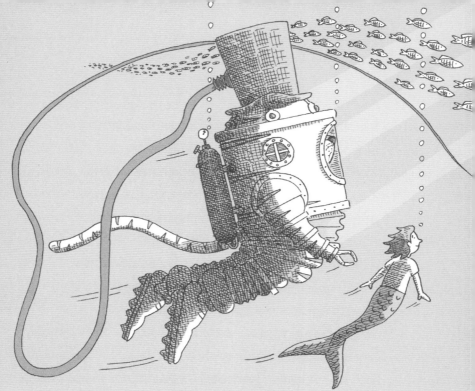

'Of course Betsy can go with you,'
said Mum, 'and then would you like to
join us for supper tonight? We, and
my sister, Coral, and her son, Floss
Grimm, are going to the Mermaid
Diner.'

'That would be a pleasure,' said
Mr Tiger.

'But how can Mr Tiger eat when

he's wearing the diving suit?' asked Betsy.

'The diner is in the starfish cave which isn't underwater,' said Mum.

Betsy swam with Mr Tiger to his submarine. She was surprised to find that although it looked small on the outside, it was enormous on the inside and very comfortable. Betsy wriggled out of her mermaid suit, fluffed up her dress and checked her golden seahorse necklace was round her neck.

'This is fantastic,' said Betsy,

looking round the submarine. 'Why did you have it built?'

Mr Tiger took off his diving suit, gave his orange striped coat a good shake and brushed his top hat.

'Tigers have their secrets and their whiskers, their tales and their tails,' he said. 'Now, Princess Albee's wedding has been brought forward and is to take place a week tomorrow, next Wednesday.'

'Wednesday is my favourite day,' said Betsy.

'There isn't much time and you have to go to Gongalong Island to be fitted for your bridesmaid's dress.'

'Oh, wow!' said Betsy. 'Will I have new shoes too?'

'Yes,' said Mr Tiger. 'New shoes, gloves and a tiara.'

He went to the fridge and brought

out a tub of Dad's Knickerbocker
Glory ice cream. He helped them both
to three large scoops.

Betsy licked her spoon. 'This
tastes of home,' she said a little
wistfully.

'Brave hearts,' said Mr Tiger.
'Brave hearts are what one needs.
You've met the sea pig?'

'Yes,' said Betsy.

'And...?'

'I don't much like him. He has a tiny seahorse called Silly Sausage, who seems unhappy and lives in a silver teapot without a lid.'

Mr Tiger took out his pocket-watch and gazed at it. 'The situation is worse than I thought,' he said. 'And time is not on our side.'

Betsy, who was on her second scoop of ice cream, said, 'Are we going to have an adventure?'

'That is very likely,' said Mr Tiger. 'In fact, I would say it has already begun. There is trouble under the sea, and we have only a few days to sort it out.'

'Crumble cakes!' said Betsy. 'I knew it.'

'This all started long ago,' said

Mr Tiger, tucking his pocket-watch safely away.

'There once was an enormous octopus who came to live here when he was rubbed off the map of the world. All was peaceful between the mer-people and the octopus. They muddled along — until the sea pig arrived. And then...'

Mr Tiger paused.

'Don't stop,' said Betsy. 'What happened?'

Mr Tiger had a twinkle in his eye.

'It's just come to me. It's not Pudding Pie that's the heart of the problem,' said Mr Tiger mysteriously. 'It's Silly Sausage and the silver teapot.'

·← 8 →·

You may be wondering what was happening meanwhile on the island left off the map of the world.

Quite a lot, for Dad had taken the plunge, so to speak. He hadn't dived into the blue sea — to be honest, he hated putting his head underwater. But he had employed Mr Walrus, a builder, to start work on the tall windy house and café.

Mr Walrus had taken many measurements and hummed and

ahhed. He said what Dad wanted was
nearly impossible. Then he said that
he might — with a push and squeeze
— be able to do it. He demanded
this, he demanded that, and finally
he started work. Mr Walrus and his
carpenter knocked holes here, there
and everywhere. There were so many
holes that the house looked like a

lump of holey cheese. Dad had to close the café. He had to move out of the tall windy house. Just when he thought things couldn't get worse, Mr Walrus and the carpenter left to go on a fishing trip somewhere on the map of the world.

The long, the short and the middle of it was that Dad was left in a right pickle. Or rather, he was left in a tall windy house made even windier because it was full of holes.

'Thank goodness Betsy isn't here to see this mess,' he said to himself.

He was scratching his head, wondering what to do for the best when Mr Tiger's ship loomed out of a sea fret and docked in the harbour. Of course, you know that Mr Tiger wasn't on board, but the Gongalong acrobats were. They were sad to

hear Dad's tale of woe and to see the muddle that the builder and his carpenter had made.

The chief Gongalong said, 'I don't know if Mr Tiger ever told you, Alfonso, but we Gongalong acrobats are rather good at building things.'

'Even if you are, how would I ever repay you?'

'There might be a way,' said the chief Gongalong. 'We have a problem and if you could solve it, we'd do your building work in exchange.'

The other Gongalongs nodded in agreement.

'Nothing I could do would be worth that much,' said Dad.

'Oh, how wrong you are!' the Gongalongs cried.

'No, truly,' said Dad. 'I don't have any skill you might need. I can't juggle or ride a horse bareback. I can't walk the high wire...'

'But you can make ice cream, Alfonso,' said the chief Gongalong. 'And if you could make a tasty ice cream from the yuckerberry, that would be payment enough.'

'From the what?' said Dad.

One of the acrobats went back to the ship and returned with a basket

of lime-yellow yuckerberries. They smelled of old socks.

'They are extremely smelly,' said Dad. 'Do you really want to eat them?'

The Gongalong acrobats began to sing.

'*It's as simple as simple can be,*
We don't have our bounce
Without the yuckerberr-eeee.'

The chief Gongalong explained. 'The yuckerberries have always tasted horrible, like cough medicine, only smellier. But if we don't eat them,

we lose our bounce and without our bounce we aren't acrobats. Now Princess Albee's wedding has been brought forward we need our bounce more than ever. You would be doing us a great favour if you could make them taste nice.'

Dad liked a good challenge and he set to work. He read every book on the yuckerberry tree. There was only one, so it didn't take him long. He asked the Gongalongs where it grew.

'It grows everywhere on our island,' they said.

'Do your horses mind eating it?' asked Dad.

'No, they don't,' said the Gongalongs. 'But we do.'

Dad wrote down all the answers.

Over a low heat and through many glass jars, pipes and tubes, he began

the slow process of distilling the yuckerberry juice.

If I can do this, he thought, *then the tall windy house and the café would be mermaid-friendly and Myrtle would come to stay more often.* Dad missed Mum and Betsy so much it was as if his heart had an ache that wouldn't go away.

Quietly, he worked on until the harbour-master popped his head into the kitchen.

'Have you noticed,' he said to Dad, 'that there's something strange about the sea? And the seagulls aren't too happy.'

Dad glanced out of the window.

'Oh dear,' he said. 'What does it mean?'

'Trouble with the sea creatures, I imagine,' said the harbour-master.

The sea was as stormy as stormy could be, but there was no wind. All was still as still could be. There wasn't a drop of rain. The sun shone as bright as bright could be. Only the waves argued the toss with themselves.

·← 9 →·

The Mermaid Diner at the starfish cave had water seats for the mermaids to sit in, and, in case of the odd landlubber, proper seats for those with legs or paws. It was a place where Mr Tiger could take off his diving helmet and his grappling claws.

Betsy was very pleased to see her cousin, Floss Grimm. He gave her a big grin and looked just the same as when she'd last seen him. That was

the thing about Floss: he always had
a jolly air about him, as if life was a
bag of pleasant surprises.

'I've brought my school project
to show you,' he said. 'It's on sea
monsters.'

He opened his backpack and

handed Betsy a large scrapbook with all sorts of things stuck into it and falling out of it at the same time.

'How is school?' asked Betsy.

'Great,' said Floss. 'It was only Dolphin Summer School that I didn't like. We have an old turtle of a teacher now and he's jammed full of knowledge. He knows all about sea monsters and their battles. Here, look.'

He opened the scrapbook at a page about the sea pig and the giant octopus.

'Crumble cakes,' said Betsy. 'This is really interesting.'

'The sea pig is believed to have come to these waters in the fifteenth century,' said Floss Grimm. 'And the giant octopus way before that.

I don't know the date. My teacher said we would have to find that out for ourselves. I bumped into the sea pig and I helped him but he didn't seem grateful. I tried to talk to him but I couldn't understand what he was saying.'

Betsy told him about the shell and how Mum was able to understand the sea pig.

'And he understands Mum, as well,' she added.

Aunty Coral was only half-listening. She was humming along to the music playing on the jukebox.

'This is off our best album,' she said to Mr Tiger. '*The Siren Singers' Greatest Hits*. This song helped sink many a galleon, I can tell you. We're no one-hit wonder.'

To Betsy's ears, it sounded like a lullaby.

'If you don't mind,' said Mr Tiger, 'I find the music makes me sleepy...'

He yawned.

Aunty Coral laughed. 'It's getting to you, isn't it?' she said, patting Mr Tiger's paw. 'This tune could put the crew of an armada to sleep.'

She asked the waitress to turn off the music. 'Now, let's get down to the rusty nail of the problem, my stripy friend. Myrtle and I agree that something must be done to stop the trouble between the giant octopus and the sea pig.'

'You see,' said Mum, 'the sea pig thinks the octopus stole his prize seahorse, Pudding Pie.'

Mr Tiger said, 'Excuse me, but has this quarrel anything to do with the stormy sea we see before us?'

'Yes,' said Aunty Coral.

'That's the pearl of the problem,' said Myrtle. 'And the sea will only get worse. Last time...'

Floss Grimm interrupted. 'I read in a book that the last time there

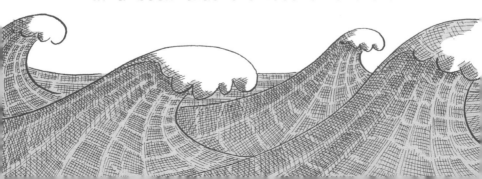

was a battle between sea monsters, they made minced mackerel out of Mermaid City.'

'In other words, it was rubble,' said Mum. 'And we don't want that happening again.'

'We don't have much time to settle this,' said Mr Tiger. 'So tomorrow, Betsy and I will visit the cantankerous octopus and get to the bottom of the problem.'

'Can I come too?' asked Floss Grimm.

'I don't see why not,' said Mr Tiger. 'If your mum will allow you.'

'As long as you do as you're told,' said Aunty Coral, who was eyeing up the sweet trolley.

'They do look good,' said Mum.

'I'll have the pink and purple delight.'

'I'll have the gold pudding and the red pudding,' said Aunty Coral. 'Oh, go on, I'll have the orange one too. I have to keep up my strength for the high notes.'

'They look mouth-watering,' said Mum. 'They're not as good as Alfonso's ice cream, but they're not bad. Betsy, which would you like?'

'Mr Tiger thinks it's Silly Sausage and the teapot that is tickling the waves into a storm,' said Betsy.

Mum and Aunty Coral looked surprised.

'How could a teapot do that?' asked Aunty Coral.

'Oh, you mean the silver teapot that the seahorse popped out of?' said Mum. 'No, that's daft.'

'I don't know,' said Aunty Coral. 'Perhaps it isn't as daft as it seems. Remember what happened between our mother and her cousin over that silver conch shell?'

Mum sighed. 'True, they never spoke to one another again. I suppose as teapots go, it's a rather nice one.'

Betsy, who was sitting next to Floss, had noticed that his ears had gone pink.

'What do you know about the teapot?' she whispered.

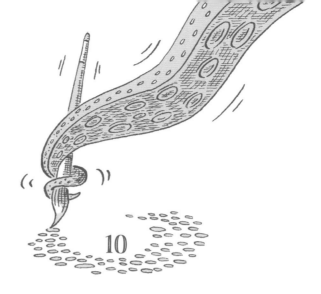

10

Every mermaid and merman had stories about the cantankerous octopus who lived in the mouth of the treasure seekers' cave to the left of the oyster beds. None of the mer-people had been near him for hundreds of years, but the tales they told had made him into a grumpy old monster of the deep. Betsy imagined his cave would be dark and gloomy. But when they turned the corner to the left of the oyster bed, there was the octopus with four brushes in his tentacles. He'd left two tentacles free. In the seventh was a palette and he was busy painting a picture. His eighth tentacle, Betsy noticed, disappeared into the mouth of the treasure seekers' cave.

When you think someone or something is going to be ... well, cantankerous, and then you find that they aren't, or it isn't, it's quite a surprise. True, the octopus was enormous. His tentacles were long and there were eight of them, so that wasn't much of a surprise. The surprise was the rocks surrounding his cave. They were painted with pictures of fish, mermaids and seahorses. They were works of art. The octopus was humming to himself. He stood back and looked at his work with one eye half-shut. He opened both eyes wide

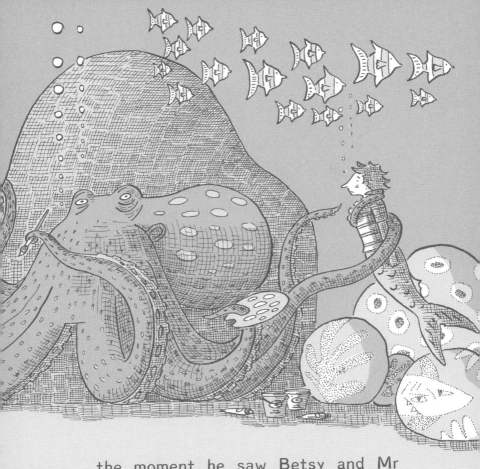

the moment he saw Betsy and Mr Tiger. Floss stayed well back. The octopus, without turning to look in his direction, dropped a paintbrush and shot out a tentacle to wrap round Floss Grimm. Then he carried on

painting as if nothing had happened.

'That's beautiful,' said Betsy, admiring the painting and trying not to sound as if she was worried that this enormous creature was holding tight to Floss.

She looked carefully at the paintings. They were so detailed and all done with tiny little dots of colour. The octopus didn't answer, and Betsy wondered whether it would have been sensible to have brought Mum's shell with her.

But then, the octopus said, 'It's my life's work. I used to keep all my paints and brushes close at tentacle in a beautiful teapot until this young upstart —' he shook the tentacle that was holding Floss — 'saw fit to whisk it away to the sea pig.'

Floss tried to speak but only succeeded in making a gurgling sound.

'I am Betsy K Glory,' said Betsy, thinking it might be polite to introduce herself before asking to have Floss back. 'You speak English very well,' she added. 'Are you a prince in disguise?' She was remembering that when she'd first met Princess Albee, the princess had been a toad.

'No, I am an octopus. I have nine brains and I am immensely clever. I also have three hearts, two of which have recently been broken. The first by the loss of my silver teapot, the second by the loss of Silly Sausage, who lived in the teapot. My third heart, you will be pleased to know, is in fine condition.'

'I'm glad to hear it,' said Mr Tiger,

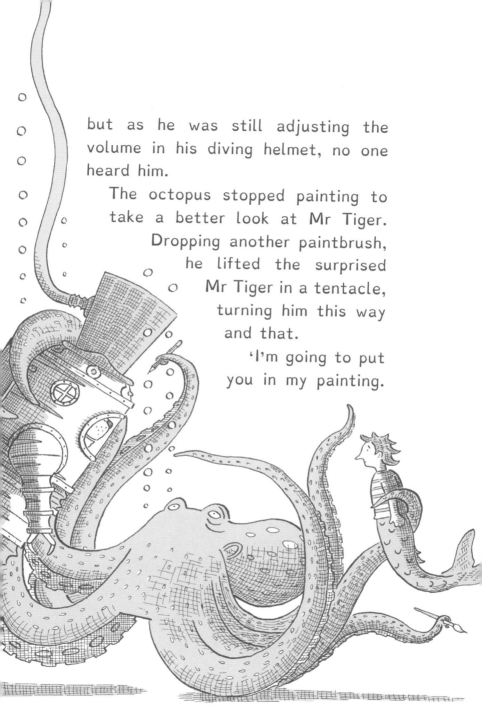

but as he was still adjusting the volume in his diving helmet, no one heard him.

The octopus stopped painting to take a better look at Mr Tiger. Dropping another paintbrush, he lifted the surprised Mr Tiger in a tentacle, turning him this way and that.

'I'm going to put you in my painting.

I've seen many sights in my long life, but a tiger in a diving suit is a thing of wonder.' He put Mr Tiger down on a rock close by. 'Please stand still.'

He took up a pencil and started to draw and paint, balancing the palette in his rippling tentacles, while still clutching Floss Grimm tightly.

'We were wondering,' said Mr Tiger, as he posed for his portrait, 'if there is any way we could persuade you and the sea pig to see tentacle to tail.'

'What is he saying?' said the octopus to Betsy. 'All his words are bubbles.'

Betsy too had difficulty hearing what Mr Tiger was saying, but she understood enough. She explained.

'No,' said the octopus. 'The sea

pig has taken my silver teapot and my Silly Sausage.'

'And you have taken his Pudding Pie,' gurgled Mr Tiger. 'Do you think you might each give something back?'

The octopus didn't understand Mr Tiger's burbling, but said, 'No,' anyway.

'What if the sea pig could be persuaded to give Silly Sausage back and we held a race to decide who will own the silver teapot?' said Mr Tiger with Betsy's help.

'A race, you say?' the octopus said, as though Mr Tiger's words were suddenly crystal clear. He thought for a moment then let go of Floss, who quickly darted out of reach.

Mr Tiger nodded. 'Yes,' he burbled. 'Over the sticks.'

The octopus pointed to Floss. 'It's your fault,' he said.

'I didn't do anything,' said Floss Grimm. 'I made a mistake, that's all. I was only trying to be helpful.'

The octopus blew some bubbles. 'I wouldn't race Silly Sausage. She's a hopeless jumper, she has no form. I will race Princess Sharky. She's one of the finest thoroughbreds in my stable. But I will only race her on the condition that the teapot is the prize.'

'First,' said Mr Tiger, 'the seahorses must each be returned to their rightful owners. Agreed?'

'What's he saying?' said the octopus again. 'I don't understand.'

'Yes, you do,' said Mr Tiger and Betsy together.

'Why do you want Silly Sausage back if she's so hopeless?' said Betsy.

'It's the right and the wrong of the thing,' said the octopus. 'I want Silly Sausage because she was stolen from me.'

'What will you do with her?' asked Floss.

'Oh, most probably keep her in the teapot where I found her. She cleans my paintbrushes, otherwise she's of no value to me.'

'In that case, may I have her, please?' said Betsy. 'I'll race her.'

·← 11 →·

'Why did you take the silver teapot to the sea pig?' Betsy asked Floss.

They were swimming with Pudding Pie back to the sea pig's galleon by way of Myrtle's house. There was something there that Mr Tiger needed.

'The more important question is how are you going to train Silly Sausage?' said Floss, while they waited in Mum's garden for Mr Tiger. 'If the sea pig will give her to us, that is.'

'You haven't answered my question,' said Betsy. 'And I asked first.'

'All right,' said Floss. 'It *might* have happened when I was on the way home from school. The water was murky, but I saw the sea pig pulling at something. I didn't understand what he was saying but he made it  clear that whatever it was was stuck.'

'How did he make it clear?' said Betsy.

Floss acted the part of the sea pig pointing with his webbed foot.

'Now I think about it, I *might* have seen the tip of a very big tentacle. I just closed my eyes and pulled. And the thing came unstuck and turned out to be a teapot. It was as easy as that. The sea pig swam away with it and I was fed up that I didn't speak sea pig and then I forgot all about it.'

Mr Tiger rejoined them. 'Floss,' he said, 'I can see it was a mistake. There is no point thinking backwards.

We have to move forward.'

'Your turn,' said Floss to Betsy. 'How're you going to train the seahorse?'

'Once I have Silly Sausage, I'm sure I'll know what to do,' said Betsy.

Though she wasn't certain if that was true. She wasn't sure about the rights and wrongs of mermaid/seahorse life. She'd done what she and Dad would have done on land — taken pity on an unhappy creature. What future did the little seahorse have with a giant octopus who didn't want her?

The sea pig let out grunts and honks of delight when he saw Pudding Pie. He invited them into the galleon and called for tea.

Mr Tiger had sensibly borrowed

Mum's shell. He managed to make it fairly clear that they had come to collect Silly Sausage and that the octopus had agreed to a race. The owner of the winning seahorse would receive the teapot.

The sea pig didn't seem at all keen on the idea. The teapot was his — no buts or tuts.

Mr Tiger gave him one of his furious glares and even through the glass of the diving helmet, it was enough to make the sea pig's scales stand on end.

'You are a huge sea pig,' said Mr Tiger. 'The octopus is enormous. Mermaids and mermen

are neither huge nor enormous, and seahorses are tiny. You all live under the sea together and a battle is out of the question. The seahorse race is to make Mermaid City safe and to put a full stop to this argument. I will take the teapot to my submarine meanwhile and keep it there.'

The sea pig clung to the teapot and Mr Tiger handed the shell to Betsy while he used his grappling claws to uncurl the sea pig's webbed feet. He snorted and honked in fury.

'What's he saying?' asked Floss.

'He wants to know which seahorse the octopus is going to race,' said Betsy. 'I told him Princess Sharky. The sea pig says Pudding Pie will beat her.'

Finally, the sea pig agreed to let

Silly Sausage go with the teapot.
He snorted when Betsy said she was
going to enter her in the race too.

They left, Mr Tiger holding tight to
the teapot with his grappling claws.

Behind them on the galleon, the
sea pig moaned to himself.

It didn't occur to Betsy to ask Silly Sausage why she liked living in a teapot. Betsy might have done if she could, but she didn't speak seahorse.

'We leave seahorse training to the octopus and the sea pig,' said Mum when Betsy returned home with Silly Sausage. 'They've done it for centuries. They have a way with seahorses.'

'Oh. I thought it might be easy,' said Betsy.

It wasn't.

The sea had become a lot calmer, which everyone took to be a good sign. The race was three days away and the octopus and the sea pig had begun their training sessions. It was fun to watch and Betsy needed all the tips she could get. At a certain grunt or a whistle, the seahorses would jump over rocks and piles of shells. Then they would potter on as only seahorses can, which is rather slowly.

Meanwhile, Betsy was trying to get Silly Sausage to come out of the teapot.

'Shake her out,' suggested Floss Grimm.

'I don't want to,' said Betsy. 'It might frighten her.'

Just then, Mr Tiger came by in his diving suit to say that he had to return to land for a short time but would be back soon.

'Can I come with you and see Dad?' asked Betsy.

'What about Silly Sausage?' said Mum.

'I'll take her with me,' said Betsy.

'Or I could look after her,' said Floss.

'I think I'd rather take her with me. You don't mind if I go, do you, Mum? It's just that...'

'Of course not,' said Mum.

'We'll be back in two days, ready for the race,' said Mr Tiger. 'And then on with all speed to Gongalong Island for last minute preparations for the wedding.'

'It doesn't leave much time to

train your seahorse,' said Floss.

'I'll work on it while I'm away,' said Betsy.

'Perfect,' said Mr Tiger. 'I'll be back to collect you in an hour.'

Betsy said goodbye to Floss then went to find Mum. She was staring out of the kitchen window.

'Are you sure you'll be all right while I go and see Dad?' said Betsy.

'Come here,' said Mum, 'and give me a hug. I think it's a very good idea. I was thinking about your seahorse and the teapot. It reminds me of an old mermaids' tale.'

'I love stories,' said Betsy. 'I think I could live off stories.'

Mum laughed. And sitting on the sofa, she told Betsy the story of The Prince and the Mermaid.

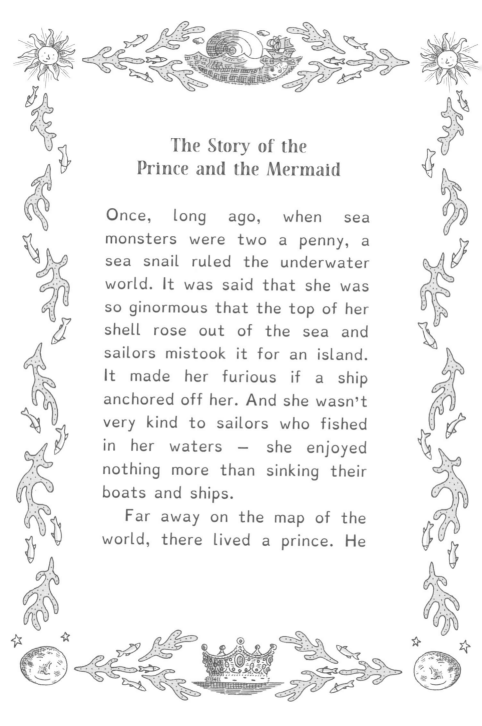

The Story of the Prince and the Mermaid

Once, long ago, when sea monsters were two a penny, a sea snail ruled the underwater world. It was said that she was so ginormous that the top of her shell rose out of the sea and sailors mistook it for an island. It made her furious if a ship anchored off her. And she wasn't very kind to sailors who fished in her waters — she enjoyed nothing more than sinking their boats and ships.

Far away on the map of the world, there lived a prince. He

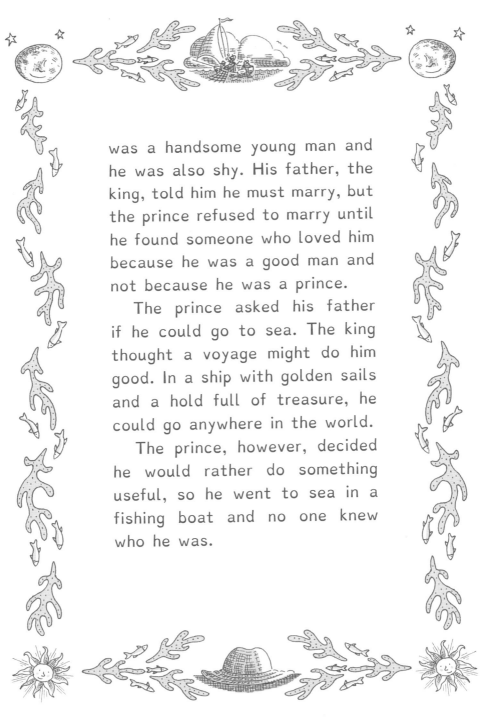

was a handsome young man and he was also shy. His father, the king, told him he must marry, but the prince refused to marry until he found someone who loved him because he was a good man and not because he was a prince.

The prince asked his father if he could go to sea. The king thought a voyage might do him good. In a ship with golden sails and a hold full of treasure, he could go anywhere in the world.

The prince, however, decided he would rather do something useful, so he went to sea in a fishing boat and no one knew who he was.

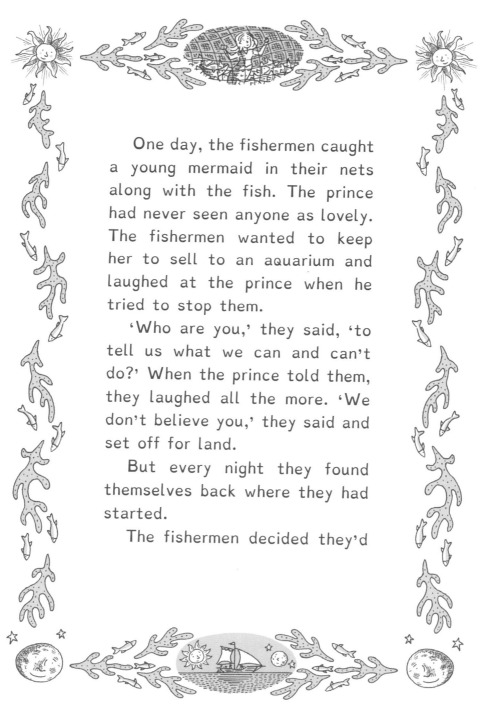

One day, the fishermen caught a young mermaid in their nets along with the fish. The prince had never seen anyone as lovely. The fishermen wanted to keep her to sell to an aquarium and laughed at the prince when he tried to stop them.

'Who are you,' they said, 'to tell us what we can and can't do?' When the prince told them, they laughed all the more. 'We don't believe you,' they said and set off for land.

But every night they found themselves back where they had started.

The fishermen decided they'd

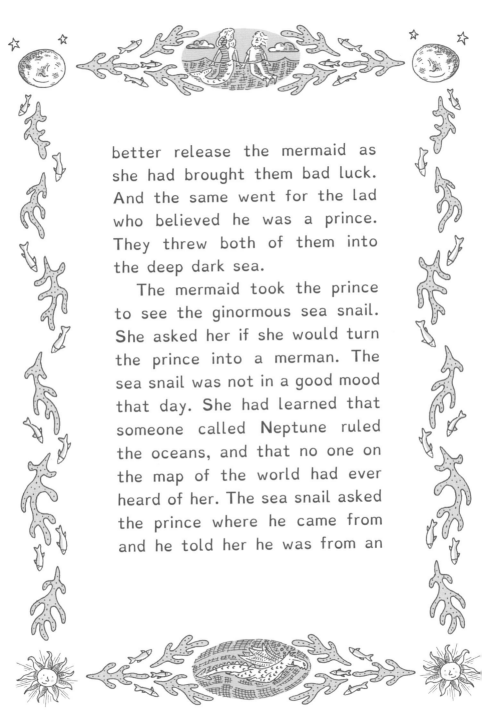

better release the mermaid as she had brought them bad luck. And the same went for the lad who believed he was a prince. They threw both of them into the deep dark sea.

The mermaid took the prince to see the ginormous sea snail. She asked her if she would turn the prince into a merman. The sea snail was not in a good mood that day. She had learned that someone called Neptune ruled the oceans, and that no one on the map of the world had ever heard of her. The sea snail asked the prince where he came from and he told her he was from an

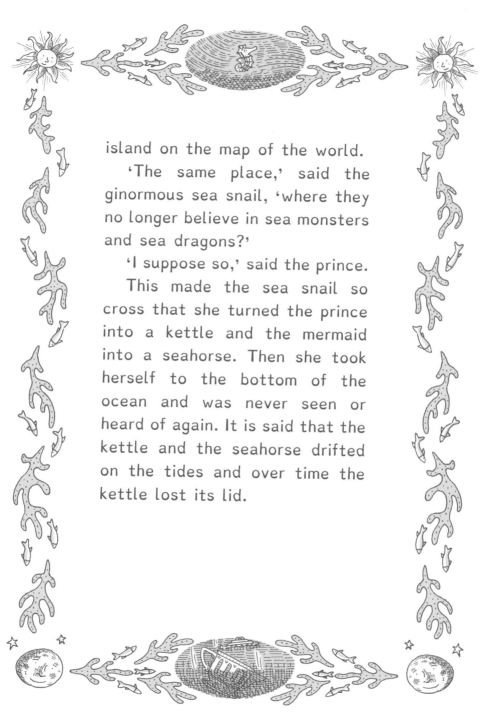

island on the map of the world.

'The same place,' said the ginormous sea snail, 'where they no longer believe in sea monsters and sea dragons?'

'I suppose so,' said the prince.

This made the sea snail so cross that she turned the prince into a kettle and the mermaid into a seahorse. Then she took herself to the bottom of the ocean and was never seen or heard of again. It is said that the kettle and the seahorse drifted on the tides and over time the kettle lost its lid.

'A kettle?' said Betsy. 'Is that it? I think that's unfair on the prince and the mermaid. Where's the happy-ever-after ending?'

·← 13 →·

Alfonso Glory had tried many experiments with the yucker-berries. It turned out to be far harder than he'd thought to distil the juice from the fruit. He had brought out all his copper pots and pans. He'd made a machine of sorts from them and powered it by pedalling his ice-cream delivery bicycle.

Every morning, Alfonso said to himself, 'Today will be the day I make the yuckerberries taste delicious.'

And every day, no matter what he did, they tasted of old socks. Alfonso began to feel defeated by the berry. The Gongalongs tried to be upbeat as they tasted yet another ice cream that was just a little less revolting than the one he'd made the day before. But the expressions on their dear little faces told Dad it was still as bad as ever it was.

When Betsy and Mr Tiger arrived at the island left off the map of the world, they found Dad pedalling his bike and going nowhere. Pans whirled and pipes gurgled. The machine had taken over all of what had been the café. Dad sighed. He had to admit things were not looking good.

He was so thrilled to see Betsy and
Mr Tiger walk into the café that
he accidentally knocked the speed-
control switch on the machine.

Unaware of what he'd done, he
rushed to lift Betsy off her feet and
hug her. This was a little difficult as
she was holding a teapot. She smelled
of sea and toast. That was because

Mr Tiger and Betsy had eaten toast in the submarine as they'd travelled to the island left off the map of the world.

Dad had put Betsy down and Mr Tiger had shaken Alfonso's hand before Betsy thought to ask what had happened to the café and where all the holes had come from. Suddenly, there was an alarming rumble from the machine. It shivered and shook the copper pots and pans — *jug-a-jug-a-jug-a*. And before you could say 'smelly socks' the large glass jar was full of bubbling, boiling yuckerberry juice. The more it boiled, the less slime-green it became. Bright, lime-green juice started to drip into the copper pan. The pan spun round and round until the juice turned into bright, lime-green candyfloss which the contraption tipped into the ice cream. Then the machine came to a grinding stop.

'Crumble cakes,' said Betsy.

The lid on the largest copper pan flew off, making another hole in the café wall.

'Oh dear,' said Dad. 'That's done

it. I must have knocked the machine's control switch on to top speed. It looks pretty broken to me.' He opened the freezer on his ice-cream bike and peered inside. He brought out a cone and put a dollop of bright, lime-green ice cream in it. 'It's a better colour,' he said. He sniffed and sniffed again. It didn't smell anything like old socks; in fact, it had a rather fresh, lemony scent. And before he could say, 'No, don't...' Betsy had tasted it.

'Wowser and wow!' said Betsy. 'It fizzes in the mouth. It tastes of...'

The Gongalongs appeared silently from nowhere. They stared at Betsy, waiting for her to say it was revolting. But she didn't.

She said, 'This, Dad, is up there with the wishable delicious Gongalongberry ice cream you made.'

'It doesn't taste like old socks?'

'No,' said Betsy. 'Why should it? It tastes of lemony-lime.'

The Gongalongs were surprised to hear Betsy say that.

'Lime? Not slime?' asked one.

'That would be revolting,' said Betsy. 'No one could eat an ice cream that tasted of old socks and slime.'

Three of the Gongalongs bravely stepped forward to try the ice cream for themselves.

'It tastes of lemons and limes, mangos and ... sherbet,' said Betsy. She took another mouthful. And another and another. 'Oh — and a little bit of ginger as well.'

The Gongalongs agreed the ice cream was delicious. But still they found it hard to believe it had been made out of yuckerberries.

'The proof is in the eating,' said Mr Tiger, leading Betsy outside. 'Now, jump, Betsy.'

'Why?' asked Betsy.

'Jump,' said the Gongalongs.

Betsy handed the teapot to Dad.

'I'm not that good at jumping,' she said.

'Jump,' called Mr Tiger and the Gongalongs together. 'Just jump, Betsy K Glory.'

And jump she did.

14

All that could be seen of Betsy were her shoes, for her head was in the clouds. She returned to the ground and before anyone could stop her, she jumped again.

'Is it safe?' asked Dad, looking worried.

'If she didn't have bounce, it wouldn't be,' said Mr Tiger. 'But as you can see, she has bounce aplenty.'

Betsy landed, jumped and immediately disappeared into the

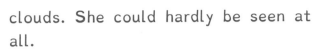

clouds. She could hardly be seen at all.

'How do I stop?' she asked as she came down to earth again.

'Bend your knees,' called the Gongalongs.

She did, but that had the effect of making her go even higher than she had before.

'Well done, Alfonso,' said the Gongalong acrobats, throwing their pointy hats in the air.

Down Betsy came and up Betsy went. And down and up. And down and up. And at last, Mr Tiger took his umbrella and hooked the handle round Betsy's ankle as she was on her way up again. He pulled her gently to the ground.

'I was sort of getting the hang of

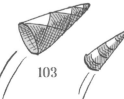

it,' she said. 'Do I really have
to stop?'

'Yes, you do,' said Mr
Tiger. 'This ice cream is
only for the use of the
Gongalongs. Imagine if
everybody was jumping
up and down.

There would, you know, be no end to the matter.'

Dad was still holding the teapot. Looking into it he saw a seahorse.

'Hello,' said Dad to the seahorse. Then, as Betsy joined him, a bit out of breath, he said, 'Do you know there's a seahorse swimming about in the teapot?'

'Yes,' said Betsy. 'Did you see how high I jumped?'

'It's strange,' said Dad. 'I thought I heard her say...'

But Betsy was too full of bounce to hear him.

·← 15 →·

Betsy left the teapot with Dad, who went to the galley of the blue-and-white striped ship to make Cherry Plum Delight ice cream for supper.

'It's good to meet you,' said Dad into the teapot. 'Do you have a name?'

'My name is Layla Rose,' said the seahorse.

'That's a pretty name,' said Dad.

'I wasn't always a seahorse,' said Layla Rose.

'What were you?' asked Dad.

Somewhere on deck a cabin door banged. The sound frightened the little seahorse and she hid in the spout of the teapot.

Dad waited. That was the thing about Dad — he was very patient. It's what Mum loved most about him.

'Hello?' he said. Then he thought that he might have spoken too loudly.

So he whispered into the spout. 'My name is Alfonso Glory.'

'My name now is Silly Sausage,' said the seahorse. 'It's my racing name.'

Betsy came into the galley and found Dad speaking into the spout of the teapot.

'Who are you talking to?' she said.

'Layla Rose,' said Dad.

'Who's that?' asked Betsy.

'Your seahorse, Layla Rose, who else?'

'No, Dad, that's Silly Sausage,' said Betsy. 'She's a racing seahorse and she is going to be in a race. If I can get her to come out of the teapot, that is.'

'She's shy,' said Dad. 'She doesn't like loud noises. She said her real name is Layla Rose and she was something else before she became a seahorse.'

Betsy stared at her dad, a puzzled expression on her face. This was a whole other side of him that she'd never seen before.

'How do you understand what she's saying?' she asked.

'Oh, you know,' said Dad. 'I suppose I must have become quite good at communicating with sea creatures, being with your mum.'

'Purrfect,' said Mr Tiger as he came into the galley. 'I always knew you were a dark horse, Alfonso, but I never knew you were a seahorse whisperer.'

Betsy bent over the teapot and looked inside, the tiny golden seahorse on the chain round her neck sparkling.

'I would really like to know why Layla Rose is so fond of this teapot,' she said.

To Betsy's amazement, the seahorse's head appeared and she made a tiny clicking sound.

Dad said, 'Layla Rose asks where your golden seahorse necklace came from. Oh, just a mo...' He listened to the seahorse again, then added, 'Were you given it, and if so by whom? I told her you were given it by Princess Albee. Layla Rose thinks you might be able to help her, but only if she has the lid of the teapot. Otherwise, you mustn't even think of it.'

'I don't understand,' said Betsy.

Dad put his ear to the spout.

'She says that if you could find the lid of the teapot, she would run the race for you with all her might.'

'Where is the lid?' asked Betsy.

'Layla Rose thinks it's in the treasure seekers' cave. She said something about a giant octopus. I don't like the sound of that one little bit.'

'Interesting,' said Mr Tiger. 'Where in the cave?'

Dad shrugged. 'She doesn't say. But without the lid, she won't race, no matter what. With the lid she says she would win.'

'Crumble cakes,' said Betsy. 'Why is the lid so important?'

Dad listened to what Layla Rose had to say.

'She says she was once a mermaid and in love with a prince. Then a ginormous sea snail changed him into a teapot and her into a seahorse,' said Dad. 'Myrtle told me an old mermaids' tale very much like that, but the prince was changed into a kettle. Anyway, it's just a story.'

'Mum told me that story too,' said Betsy.

Layla Rose growled.

'Oh,' said Dad, listening again.

'It's not just a story, it's true. She says the sea creatures don't always understand each other and over time they've got the story wrong. And ... and she says your golden seahorse is magical and could change the teapot back into the prince. But she must have the lid first, or the prince might come back headless and that would never do.'

Mr Tiger took out his pocket-watch. 'Then we must find the lid, pronto,' he said. 'And Layla Rose must win the race or she'll lose her teapot to the octopus or the sea pig.'

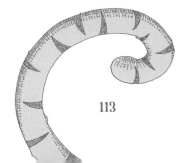

·← 16 →·

Layla Rose suggested that if Mr Tiger asked the giant octopus nicely he might allow Betsy to go into the cave.

'Not a bad suggestion,' said Mr Tiger.

'It's a terrible suggestion!' said Dad. 'Not Betsy. What about Floss Grimm? Can't he go into the cave and find the lid?'

'It wouldn't be safe for Floss Grimm,' said Mr Tiger. 'Not after what happened the last time.'

'I'll do it,' said Betsy bravely.

'Surely there's someone else who is up for the job? Betsy is small and...'

'That's exactly why she's perfect,' said Mr Tiger, putting a paw on Dad's shoulder. 'I'll be close by. I won't let anything bad happen to Betsy.'

'But how can you stop a giant octopus?' said Dad.

'I will make sure that he is never out of my sight. And there's this.' Mr Tiger opened a cupboard and took out a torch attached to a strap. 'Betsy can wear it on her head so that she can see where she's going. Now, my dear Alfonso, stop worrying. As you can speak to Layla Rose, we'll leave her and the teapot with you.'

Dad didn't look happy. 'It's all happening underwater and I don't mean to be...' He stopped. 'Neither of you is used to being underwater.'

'I have my golden seahorse,' said Betsy. 'Layla Rose says it's magical.'

'Yes,' said Dad. 'But we don't know what its magical powers might be.'

'A worthy point,' said Mr Tiger. 'And one that we need an answer to as soon as possible. I'll ask some of the Gongalong acrobats if they would go through the tunnel to Gongalong Island and put that question to Princess Albee.'

'Shouldn't we wait for the reply before you leave?' said Dad, who always erred on the cautious side of life.

'No,' said Mr Tiger. 'Sometimes you have to seize the moment and now is that moment. Brave hearts, Alfonso, brave hearts.'

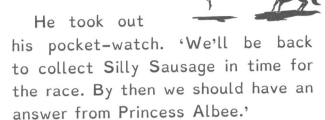

He took out his pocket-watch. 'We'll be back to collect Silly Sausage in time for the race. By then we should have an answer from Princess Albee.'

They had lunch and afterwards Mr Tiger made a short but important speech to boost the Gongalongs' spirits. Then Betsy and Mr Tiger climbed into the submarine.

'Not long, my gutsy friends,' said Mr Tiger, 'until we're back. And not long until we give a star performance at Princess Albee's wedding.'

It was a truly uplifting speech and the acrobats threw their pointy hats in the air and shouted, 'Hurray!' from the bottom of their boots to the tops of their voices.

Dad, holding the teapot, waved goodbye to Betsy and Mr Tiger.

He watched anxiously as Mr Tiger's top hat vanished from view, the hatch closed and the submarine disappeared beneath the waves.

'Cheer up, Alfonso,' said the Gongalongs. 'Remember, today we start work and we'll soon have your house mermaid-friendly.'

Mum was delighted to have Betsy back so soon and not at all surprised to hear that Dad could talk to a seahorse.

'He was always rather good at things like that,' she said.

Floss Grimm, on the other hand, was disappointed that Betsy hadn't brought Silly Sausage with her.

'Does Uncle Alfonso know how to train a seahorse?' he said. 'I mean —

119

seahorse racing is a difficult sport.'

Betsy had no idea if Dad knew about seahorse racing or not.

'The important thing is he can speak to Layla Rose and we can't.'

It was Mum's suggestion that when they had found the teapot lid, Floss should go with Betsy on the submarine to collect Layla Rose in time for the race. This cheered him up no end.

'I'll be able to have Uncle Alfonso's ice cream again,' he said.

That evening, Betsy told Floss and Mum about Dad's yuckerberry ice cream and how it gave you bounce. And that Mr Tiger had said it was only for the use of the Gongalong acrobats.

'Mr Tiger is right,' said Mum as

she tucked Betsy up in bed. 'The yuckerberry ice cream mustn't be eaten by anyone other than the acrobats. Can you imagine what would happen if everyone ate it?'

Betsy closed her eyes. First she thought about her bridesmaid dress, then her shoes and tiara, and finally a picture popped into her head of everyone being able to jump as high as the moon. She was giggling as she fell asleep.

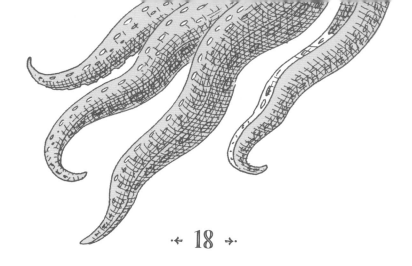

·+ **18** +·

The following morning, Mr Tiger, Betsy, Mum and Floss Grimm arrived bright and early at the treasure seekers' cave.

'We are here...' said Mr Tiger. This came out as *gurgle, burble, pop-pop.*

Mum burst out laughing and took over. 'We're here to ask if I might look in your cave. We hope to find the lid of the teapot that Silly Sausage lives in.'

'I don't want any mermaid snooping about in my cave,' said the octopus.

'Go away, I'm busy.' With one of his tentacles he gave Princess Sharky a push. 'Faster,' he said. 'We haven't got all day for you to get over this jump.'

Floss Grimm, who had stayed in the background, swam forward.

'Not you again,' said the octopus.

'Yes, me,' said Floss. 'I thought you should know that it's a very fine lid. It would make the teapot more special — it would be a proper teapot. And the lid is in your cave.'

'Are you sure? How do I know this isn't a lie disguised as a worm to tempt me? I don't eat worms, but I could eat...'

Mr Tiger clutched Floss in his grappling claw to stop the octopus from snatching him.

'...ice cream,' said the octopus.

'And I have heard that Mr Alfonso Glory's ice cream is the best on or off the map of the world.'

'I could arrange for a tub or two to be brought to you,' said Mr Tiger. His words came out as *pop-pop, gargle, pop*.

'What is he warbling about?' said the octopus, shrugging his tentacles.

Floss explained.

'We are talking about *the* Mr Alfonso Glory who married a mermaid?' said the octopus. 'And you are offering me his ice cream?'

'Yes,' said Betsy. 'And once we've found the lid the teapot will be whole again.'

'But only if you allow my Aunty Myrtle to go into the treasure seekers' cave,' said Floss.

'I'll be quick,' said Mum.

'No,' said the octopus. 'No and doubly no.'

'But a whole teapot is better than a teapot with a bit missing,' said Floss Grimm.

'I don't know,' said the octopus. 'Perhaps you are trying to tickle my tentacles. And then steal my treasure.'

'What flavour ice cream would you like?' asked Betsy.

'I've heard the chocolate chip brownie bites are excellent. But my

second brain tells me that I should go
for the rhubarb and strawberry cream
with peach sherbet topping sundae.
I think I could eat that Monday to
Friday.'

'That's easy-peasy,' said Betsy.

'All right,' he said. 'But only you,
Betsy K Glory, can go in, as you're
not a proper mermaid. You can stay
in the cave for as long as it takes
me to count to eight. After that, you
come out.'

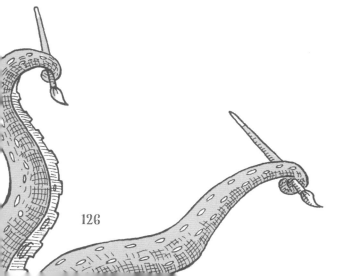

19

Betsy put the torch on her head and Mum tightened the straps.

'You will take your tentacle out of the cave while Betsy is in there,' said Mum firmly to the octopus.

'Of course,' he said. 'But only for as long as it takes me to count to eight.'

'That's not very long,' said Betsy. 'If you have as many brains as you say you do, I would have thought you might be able to count to twenty.'

'Eight is a good number — sweet, curvy and neat,' said the giant octopus.

'Shall I tell you a joke?' said Floss Grimm.

'Is it long?' said Betsy.

'No, very short. Why did nought need a belt?'

'I don't know,' said Betsy.

'So it could become eight,' said the octopus, flexing a tentacle.

Betsy was puzzled.

'Come on,' said Floss. 'A nought with a belt tied tight in the middle is an eight. Good, isn't it?'

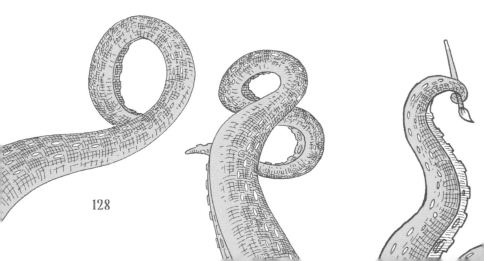

Mr Tiger felt a short speech was called for.

'Remember, Betsy, brave hearts,' he said. 'Brave hearts...'

The rest of his words were lost in his diving helmet, but Betsy got the message.

'All right,' said Betsy, switching on her torch. 'Eight it is.'

She waited until the octopus had pulled his eighth tentacle from the cave.

'One...' he said.

'Wait a second,' said Floss, wriggling to free himself from Mr Tiger's grappling claw. 'Give her a chance — she isn't even inside yet.'

Betsy sped past, careful not to touch any of his tentacles. To be honest, she really wasn't very keen

on the octopus and she didn't trust him.

'One,' he said again.

The beam of light from the torch on Betsy's head didn't do justice to the size of the cave. It was vast. If there was treasure in it, Betsy couldn't see it. The water was darkly murky and seaweed brushed against her. Not pretty seaweed, the brown kind that feels like creepy fingers. She nearly bumped into a rock standing in the middle of the cave.

What a silly place to put a rock, she thought.

'Two,' came the impatient voice of the octopus.

Betsy told herself this was no time to dilly-dally. She was there to find the lid of a teapot and there wasn't much time.

'Three.'

Betsy swam back and forth, shining her light on the muddy floor of the cave. The search was very hit and miss.

'Four.'

She found two old sea chests filled with shells. A school of fish swam out of one of them. And she thought she saw something move in the mud. Or perhaps she didn't, it was hard to tell in such a small beam of light.

'Five.'

It shouldn't really be called the treasure seekers' cave, she thought, *when there's no treasure.*

Outside the cave, the octopus said, 'Six,' loudly.

'This is not going well,' said Betsy to herself.

'Seven.'

It was then she saw it. Just as she was about to give up, below her, between two jagged rocks, she glimpsed a shimmer of silver. She swam closer. Yes! It was definitely the lid. She dived down towards it. The trouble was, it was stuck. She'd managed to wiggle it free when she saw something in the mud. Whatever it was had two gleaming eyes and they were staring at her.

But she had the lid in her hand
and she quickly swam up through
the jagged rocks as the octopus
called, 'Eight.'

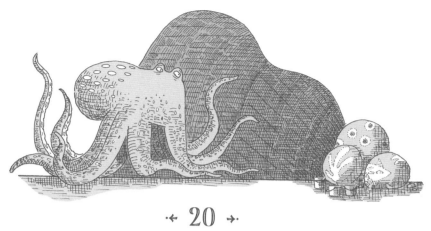

20

'Eight,' repeated the octopus.
Absolutely nothing happened. Mum was at her wit's end. In other words, she'd had enough. Floss was in a real tizzy and Mr Tiger struggled to hold him back. Mr Tiger was furious. And at last he'd found his voice.

'Where is she?' he roared at the octopus.

It could have turned out badly. But at that moment, a dazed Betsy floated out of the mouth of the treasure seekers' cave, holding the lid of the teapot. Mum swiftly swam to her and wrapped her in her arms.

'Are you hurt?' she said.

'I don't know,' said Betsy. 'I feel dizzy. But I found the lid.'

'Yes, you did,' said Mum and kissed her.

Betsy suddenly put her hand to her neck. 'Oh, no,' she said. 'It's gone!'

'What's gone?' asked Mum.

'The golden seahorse that Princess Albee gave me,' said Betsy. 'I know I had it on when I was in the cave. And now it's gone.'

Betsy was trying to stay calm, which is hard when something you love is lost.

People are said to cry over spilled

milk, which, to Betsy, seemed a pretty silly thing to do. If crying would help, she would be weeping buckets over losing her golden seahorse necklace. But there was no point, so she wasn't. Instead she made up her mind that she would go back to the cave and find it.

'That sounds exciting,' said Floss Grimm. 'I'll come with you.'

Mr Tiger purred. Then he said, 'NO.' And it was such a big **NO** that Betsy had to agree.

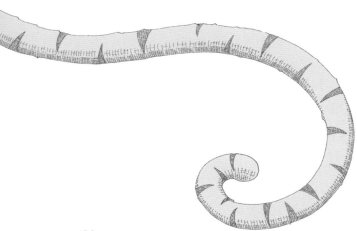

·← 21 →·

After Betsy and Mr Tiger had left, a message arrived for Dad from Septimus Plank. He asked if Dad could make the ice cream for the wedding cake with a creamy-lemony flavour. Septimus added he needed it urgently.

'Oh dear,' said Dad.

He'd only just finished making the yuckerberry ice cream and now he set to work on the mixture for the wedding cake. He was interrupted so many times by Layla Rose that he was finding it hard to concentrate.

'It's hopeless,' she said again and again. 'Betsy will never find the lid and without the lid I will have a headless prince.'

Carefully Dad wrote out the labels for the ice cream. Some said 'Yuckerberry', some said 'Wedding Cake'. He was about to stick them on the tubs when a Gongalong acrobat hurried into the galley where Dad was working.

'Alfonso,' he said, 'Mr Tiger's submarine has just surfaced.'

Dad was so excited that he grabbed the teapot and rushed to the harbour wall.

'I've been so worried,' said Dad. 'I must have four more white hairs than I did yesterday.'

Betsy gave Dad a hug. 'I found the lid,' she said.

Inside the teapot, Layla Rose jumped with joy, clicking to Dad in excitement.

'She says, drop your golden seahorse down the teapot's spout and her prince will be returned to her whole,' said Dad.

'I wish I could — but I can't,' said Betsy miserably. 'I've lost it. It fell off in the treasure seekers' cave while I was searching for the lid.'

On hearing this, Layla Rose disappeared into the spout of the teapot where she growled at Dad.

'What's she saying?' asked Betsy.

'Put the lid on the teapot and leave her and her prince in peace. It's all hopeless.'

Betsy was a feisty girl and one thing Mr Tiger had taught her was that nothing is hopeless.

'I'm not giving up,' she said, taking the teapot from Dad. 'And neither should you, Layla Rose.'

And although Layla Rose didn't understand her, Betsy felt the seahorse knew what she meant.

Dad carried Floss Grimm into the galley of Mr Tiger's ship and sat him down with his tail in a bucket.

'Can I have some ice cream, please,

Uncle Alfonso?' he asked.

'Um ... yes ... er ... wait a mo,' said Dad.

'Come on,' said Betsy, taking Dad's hand. 'I want to see what the Gongalongs have done to the café.'

'So do I,' said Mr Tiger.

'But nothing's finished yet,' said Dad. 'There's still lots to do.'

And the three of them left Floss alone in the galley. Seeing all the tubs of ice cream on the worktop, he jiggled his chair and bucket closer.

Uncle Alfonso didn't say I couldn't, he thought to himself. *And what harm is there in tasting just a little bit?* He opened one of the tubs. There was a spoon within arm's reach and with it he took a mouthful. The ice cream was delicious. Moving the tub from left to right he tried another. Then he moved another tub from right to left and tried that. And then he thought he would try them all. Suddenly he heard Mr Tiger, Betsy and Uncle Alfonso coming up the gangplank. Quickly he put the lids back on the tubs and moved them to where he thought they'd been before.

'Do you know, Uncle Alfonso,' said Floss, 'if I could eat ice cream like this every day, I wouldn't want to be anywhere but here.'

'Which tub did you taste the ice cream from?' asked Dad.

'Er — that one.' Floss pointed to the nearest tub.

'Are you sure?' asked Dad, looking worried.

'Oh, yes,' said Floss.

Mr Tiger took out his pocket-watch.

'Unfortunately, Alfonso, we have to leave with all speed. There is a race to win, two sea monsters to calm down and a wedding to attend.'

Dad took Mr Tiger aside.

'I don't know if Layla Rose will race,' he said. 'She's very down in the dumps.'

'You'd better tell her that a bargain is a bargain,' said Mr Tiger. 'It took courage to find the lid and she must win that race if she doesn't want to lose her teapot.'

Dad told her.

Betsy carried the silver teapot on to the submarine, Dad carried Floss Grimm, and Mr Tiger came last, having had a few important words with his Gongalongs about the wedding preparations.

No sooner had they left in the submarine than it was time for Dad to depart for Gongalong Island with the ice cream. He packed all the tubs in ice and then, on a rose-coloured evening, while the sun was being read a bedtime story, Alfonso Glory and the Gongalongs set sail.

·← 22 →·

The seahorse racecourse was in the middle of Mermaid City. It was a straight strip of sand, not very long, with colourful jumps leading to the finishing line. On each side were crowds of mermaids and mermen. Betsy had no idea it would be so busy. Shoals of fish circled above to watch. A row of seahorses blew their trumpets and a crab and lobster band played the shells.

There was a huge cheer when the

sea pig came on to the racecourse with Pudding Pie, who was wearing a sea-blue cape with pom-poms. She bobbed her head from side to side, greeting her fans. There was an even bigger cheer when the octopus arrived with Princess Sharky, who looked most fetching in a coral-pink cape.

Mr Tiger had hoped to have a quiet word with them before the race, though in his diving suit, and without the shell, it was tricky. Mum had said she would bring the shell, but she was nowhere to be seen. When at last he reached the sea pig and the octopus they were both cross that the silver teapot wasn't on display.

'Where is it?' said the octopus. 'Why have you hidden it from us?'

Mr Tiger tried to explain but the octopus said he had far better things to do than to listen to the watery words of a tiger in a diving suit, bubbles or no bubbles. The sea pig agreed. He had no time for Mr Tiger's splutters and gurgles, which made no sense to either of the sea monsters.

Betsy and Floss Grimm were trying
to persuade Layla Rose to come out
of the teapot. Layla Rose clicked and
growled, and Betsy wished that Dad
was there to help.

'I told you she was useless,' said
the octopus when Betsy and the
teapot joined him and the sea pig
at the starting gates.

'That seahorse couldn't win a crab race,' grunted the sea pig.

'The teapot should be at the end of the race, not the beginning,' said the octopus. 'It is the prize, after all.'

'I would rather it had no one living in it,' said the sea pig.

'Are we ready?' said the turtle, who was there to make sure everything went without a hiccup.

Finally, the two seahorses and the teapot were in the starting gates. The turtle blew his whistle, the crowd cheered and, as far as Betsy could see, nothing happened. After

a minute or so, Pudding Pie ambled
off, to a great cheer from the crowd,
followed quite casually by Princess
Sharky. She stopped to talk to fans
before taking the first jump. Layla
Rose hadn't yet appeared from
the teapot.

'I think,' said the octopus,
'that you, Betsy K Glory, are
the silly sausage for entering
the race.'

'Crumble cakes,' said Betsy to
Floss, who was trying to tip Layla
Rose out of the teapot.

'No cheating,' said the turtle.

Layla Rose hadn't moved.

'This isn't going well,' said Floss
Grimm.

The judge, a whale, was waiting at
the finishing line with his stopwatch.

The sight of him spurred on Pudding Pie and Princess Sharky, who arched their necks and tossed their heads so they would look beautiful as they ambled to the final jump.

'What are we going to do?' said Betsy. 'The race is nearly over.'

Suddenly Floss and Betsy saw Layla Rose poke her head out of the teapot and eye the two seahorses.

'She looks like a seahorse with a plan,' said Floss, hope rising within him.

Princess Sharky and Pudding Pie, who were busy chatting to their fans, didn't notice Layla Rose shooting out of the teapot.

'Go, Layla Rose, go!' cried Betsy.

Layla Rose took the hurdles in record time. Princess Sharky and Pudding Pie were so surprised when she zoomed past them that they couldn't think what to do except watch as Layla Rose jumped the final fence.

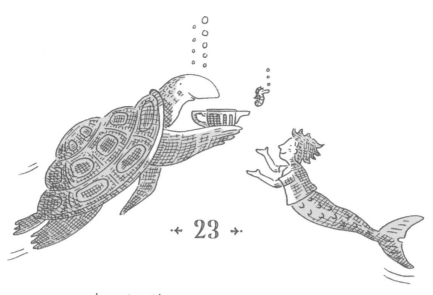

·← **23** →·

The turtle announced that the winner of the silver teapot was Layla Rose, owned and trained by Betsy K Glory.

'It cannot be!' wailed the sea pig.

'No, no!' said the octopus, beating the water with his tentacles before handing the sea pig a hanky.

'Most kind,' grunted the sea pig.

Mr Tiger approached the octopus and the sea pig. He had found Mum and she'd given him the shell so he could be understood. Sort of.

'Surely you see,' he said, 'that you two have lots in common.'

'Like what?' said the octopus.

'Like art, for instance,' said Mr Tiger.

'That's true,' said the sea pig. 'I have some very fine watercolours and I've always admired your paintings.'

'You have?' said the octopus.

'Very much,' said the sea pig.

'I have always thought your galleon to be most handsome,' said the octopus. 'You have excellent taste.'

'Would you like to come to tea and see my collection?' said the sea pig.

'Yes — I am free on Thursday,' said the octopus.

'And ... and do you think that

you might do me a
painting?' said the
sea pig.
'I think
I could,'
said the
octopus.
'But we still
don't have
the teapot.'
'I might have
another one, tucked away,' said the
sea pig. 'It's gold. We could ... share
it.'

The octopus put a tentacle round
the sea pig. 'Tea on Thursday it is,
then.'

'I think we have been silly,' said
the sea pig.

'I agree,' said the octopus.

'After all,' said the sea pig, 'there aren't that many of us sea monsters left.'

'Friends?'

'Friends.'

Mr Tiger addressed the crowd through the shell so everyone could understand him.

'Mer-people and sea creatures,' said Mr Tiger, 'the true winners of the race are the octopus and the sea pig.' The crowd roared. 'I think I speak for everyone here when I say that having you two magnificent monsters in the ocean left off the map of the world makes this place special indeed. And long may it remain so.'

The crowd applauded as the sea pig and the octopus bowed before disappearing together into the watery horizon.

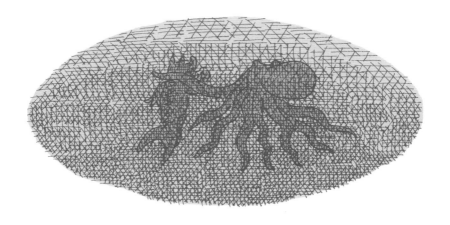

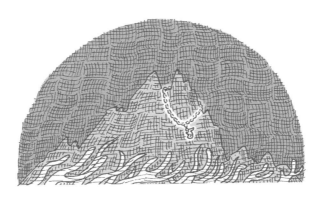

·← 24 →·

Betsy couldn't find Mum in the crowd.

'Have you seen her?' she asked Mr Tiger.

'She gave me the shell,' he said, 'but then she disappeared.' He took out his pocket-watch with his grappling claw. 'We need to leave — time is running away with the day and there are minutes to catch and hours to gather if we are to get everything done in time for the wedding.'

'We have to find Mum before we go,' said Betsy. 'And what about my seahorse necklace? We must try to turn the teapot back into the prince before we go to the wedding.'

Mr Tiger held his pocket-watch up to his diving helmet so he could see it better.

'Good,' he said. 'Very good. Come on, Myrtle is waiting for us.'

Floss Grimm swam up to them, holding the silver teapot.

'How is it your pocket-watch works underwater?' asked Floss with interest.

'Tigers have their secrets and their whiskers, their tales and their tails,' said Mr Tiger. 'Is Layla Rose back in her teapot?'

'Yes,' said Floss. 'She went straight

in as soon as she'd won the race.'

'Then all is in order,' said Mr Tiger.

'But what about my golden seahorse?' asked Betsy again.

'Come along,' said Mr Tiger. 'There's not a whisker to be lost.'

They found Mum waiting for them, just as Mr Tiger had said.

Betsy swam to her and gave her a hug.

'You missed the race, Mum — Layla Rose won.'

'I knew she would,' said Mum.

'Is there time to look for my necklace before we leave?' asked Betsy. 'Or shall we come back after the wedding?'

'Funny you should mention that,' said Mum, 'because I heard that a certain little girl with bright purple hair and the greenest of eyes and the sweetest freckled face I have ever seen had lost her golden seahorse in the treasure seekers' cave. And I heard that she was being brave about it. I also heard that a certain seahorse and a certain teapot would never be able to undo the spell cast on them by a ginormous sea snail without the golden seahorse. So, while the race was on, I took a torch and went to look for it.'

'Oh, Mum! Did you find it?'

The lid popped off the teapot as Mum held up a golden chain. Dangling from it was the magical golden seahorse.

'You did,' said Betsy. 'You found it!'

'Yes,' said Mum. 'It was caught on a jagged rock.'

'What now?' asked Floss, who had caught the lid and replaced it on the teapot.

'What now? It's up to Betsy,' said Mr Tiger, turning to her. 'Are you ready to give it away?'

Betsy held the silver teapot in one hand and her golden seahorse in the other.

'I'll get it back again, won't I?'

'Maybe,' said Floss. 'Probably.'

At that moment, a beam of light

shone through the water on to the seabed, lighting up Betsy and the teapot.

'Go on,' said Floss.

'Remember,' said Mr Tiger, 'brave hearts.'

Betsy closed her eyes and dropped the golden seahorse down the spout.

Nothing happened. Nothing at all.

'Oh,' said Betsy. 'What shall we do?'

'Wait?' suggested Mum.

'We can't,' said Mr Tiger. 'We need to be purring along. We'll have to take the teapot with us to Gongalong Island.'

'Perhaps Princess Albee can tell us about the golden seahorse's magical powers,' said Betsy, fishing her necklace out of the teapot. 'We must be doing something wrong.'

Once they were aboard the submarine it was time for bed. There was a waterbed each for Mum and Floss and hammocks for Mr Tiger and Betsy. Mr Tiger plotted the course and switched the submarine to automatic pilot.

'Tomorrow morning,' said Mr Tiger with a yawn, 'we will arrive at Gongalong Island. Sleep tight.'

And all that could be heard was the gentle purring of a tiger.

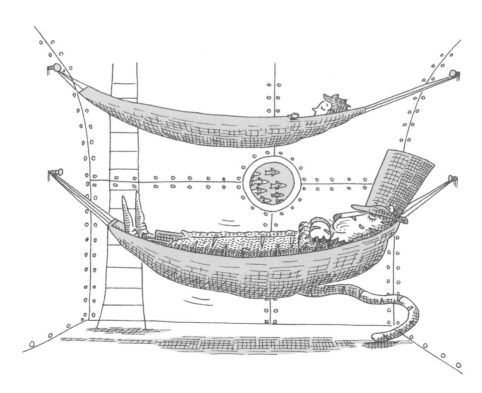

·← 25 →·

D ad had arrived on Gongalong Island to be greeted by Septimus Plank and seventeen Gongalong trainee pastry chefs.

'I might have made too much,' Dad said as the trainee pastry chefs carried the tubs of ice cream to the palace kitchen.

There, with a golden spoon, Septimus tasted the ice cream for himself. Then the seventeen trainee pastry chefs tried it.

'Oh, this is full of happy-ever-afters,' said Septimus. 'It's perfect for the ice cream wedding cake.'

He was so thrilled that he did a jig on the spot, one he had learned from the pirates on the Kettle Black, and the trainee pastry chefs threw their hats in the air.

It was then that one of the Gongalong acrobats arrived with a message for Dad.

'What's this?' said Dad.

'The answer to your question. The one about the golden seahorse,' said the Gongalong.

Dad read the note:

The golden seahorse has no
known magical powers.

'Oh dear,' said Dad. 'That's disappointing.'

'Is everything all right?' asked Septimus.

'Yes,' said Dad. 'It's nothing that stops us from making the cake.'

'Good,' said Septimus. 'Then let me show you what we are going to do with this delicious ice cream.'

The palace had an ice house and

it was there that Septimus had laid out the cake he'd baked, ready to be filled with ice cream. Dad helped him. He filled turret-shaped cake and spire-shaped cake and staircase-shaped cake.

'What is this going to be?' asked Dad.

'Wait and see,' said Septimus.

Finally, there wasn't another bit of cake that could be filled.

It was then that the seventeen Gongalong trainee pastry chefs went to work. Dad watched, amazed, as out of all the bits and pieces a magical fairy castle appeared. It was taller than Dad and looked almost too good to eat. When it was done, Septimus,

Dad and the trainee pastry chefs posed in front of it for a photo.

'Alfonso, do you think Princess Albee will like it?' asked Septimus.

'If she doesn't, then she's marrying the wrong pastry chef,' said Dad.

The Gongalongs agreed that it was the best wedding ever, a day for the history books of Gongalong Island.

It began with the arrival of Mr Tiger's submarine in the harbour. Mum, Betsy and Floss Grimm went to join Dad in the palace's water-suite which had all mod cons for mer-people. Dad had to tell them — and then Layla Rose — the disappointing news about the golden seahorse. Layla Rose told Dad she wouldn't think about it today. On such a happy occasion it was wrong to be sad.

☆ ☆

Betsy was still trying to take in the grandeur of the palace when a Gongalong seamstress came to tell her it was time to try on her bridesmaid dress. First she put on three petticoats, then the dress itself. It was ankle length with puffed sleeves, and made from the palest pink silk, embroidered with tiny silver flowers. Six little seamstresses had to use stepladders to fasten the dress at the back. The

Gongalongs, of course, are less than a quarter of the size of an average human.

Two Gongalong shoemakers brought Betsy the most beautiful pair of silver shoes that glimmered as she walked. Two Gongalong glovemakers brought a pair of elbow length lace gloves. When her hair had been brushed and a small tiara placed on her head, Betsy at last saw herself in the mirror. The golden seahorse necklace glittered and she thought she looked like a princess.

After the dress fitting came the wedding rehearsal and then everyone waited with butterflies in their tummies for the sun to go to bed. But the sun decided to stay up late and colour the sky from its paint pots of reds, purples and oranges. At last, night drew its velvet curtain over the day.

It was then that thousands of tiny fairy lights came on in the garden where the wedding was to take place, so it glimmered with pinpricks of light. The moon appeared on time wearing a gleaming gown and came to rest on the edge of the sea where it had an excellent view. Dad carried Mum to their seats with the other guests

and three Gongalong acrobats carried Floss Grimm to his.

The orchestra started to play as Princess Albee walked down a rose petal path with Betsy holding the lace train that sparkled with gems. Waiting under an arch of flowers was Septimus Plank, looking very smart in a tailcoat and a silver chef's hat. With him were his seventeen Best Men and Women, all of them trainee pastry chefs.

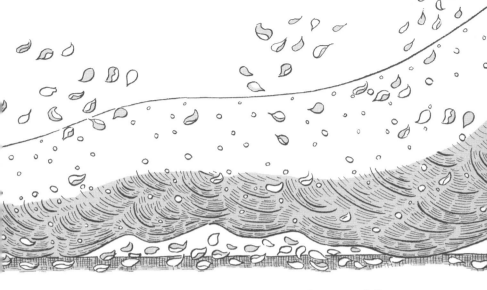

Mr Tiger performed the wedding ceremony and gave a speech about having fun. He said it was the hardest word to spell, for in those three little letters lay the secret to a happy life together.

We, the letters of the alphabet, wholeheartedly agree. And, by the by, we do love a wedding when happy words are thrown around as freely as confetti. But don't let us hold up the ceremony — on with the story.

Mr Tiger pronounced Princess Albee and Septimus Plank man and wife and the Gongalongs threw their pointy hats in the air.

Supper was served and the giant, Ivan the Bold, who had come down from the mountain, sat next to the moon at the top table.

Princess Albee rose to give a speech. She said that without the help of the moon and Ivan the Bold she most probably would still be a toad with a rather long tongue and a passion for ice cream and would never have met the love of her life. On that note, Septimus asked the seventeen trainee pastry chefs to bring out the ice cream wedding cake. The guests gasped in amazement when they saw it.

'Dad,' said Betsy, 'it's a fairy palace. I've never seen such a beautiful cake.'

Princess Albee said she had married the best pastry chef on or off the map of the world and the happy couple cut the cake. There was more than enough for everyone. Some guests had two helpings. Some had three. Ivan the Bold had ten helpings — after all, he is a giant. The orchestra played as the Gongalong acrobats put up their ladders, ready to walk a tightrope between the moon and stars.

Floss Grimm had been fidgeting in his bucket. Suddenly, he said, 'I think — even with a tail — I could jump that high.'

And to everyone's surprise he did and landed again safe and sound.

'How did you do that?' asked the wedding guests.

'Oh, I don't know. I just jumped,' said Floss. But his ears were glowing red.

Everyone started to jump and they too found themselves as high as the moon. They landed and jumped again and again.

'It's magic,' they shouted as up and down they went. 'You try,' they said to Ivan the Bold, 'go on.'

He was worried that being so big he might hurt someone on the way down.

'No you won't,' said Princess Albee. 'Have a go.'

So Ivan did. He jumped so high that he did four somersaults before landing to a great cheer.

'Oh dear,' said Dad. 'It seems

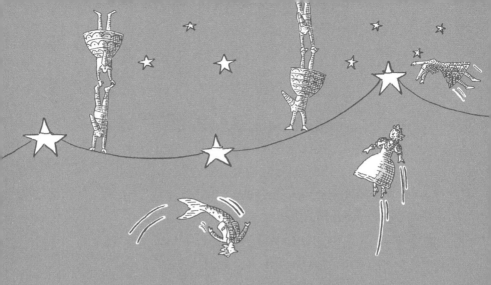

some of the yuckerberry ice cream was jumbled up with the wedding cake mixture.' Watching Floss Grimm jumping and landing, jumping and landing, Dad thought he knew exactly how it had happened.

'Never mind, Alfonso,' said Septimus, 'it couldn't have turned out better.' He turned to Princess Albee. 'Could it, my love?' and the bride and bridegroom jumped and rested a while on the moon.

'I wouldn't worry about it,' said Mr Tiger, his paw on Dad's shoulder. 'It's the purrfect end to a wedding.'

Mum put her arms round Dad and said, 'Let's give it a go, Alfonso.'

'Oh — wait a minute, there is something I have to tell you and I keep forgetting ... you see what with the wedding, the builders and the yuckerberry ice cream, the Gongalong acrobats didn't have time enough to make the tall windy house mermaid-friendly.'

'Mr Alfonso K Glory,' said Mum. 'What a wonderful muddle you are. You tried and that's all that matters.'

She took his hand and together they jumped. 'I'm a flying mermaid,' she said with delight as they came down and flew up again.

Mr Tiger, holding the silver teapot, sat tapping his cane to the music. Betsy landed beside him.

'Shall we go down to the beach?' he said, handing Betsy the teapot.

They walked along the sand. Above them the wedding guests were still jumping while the Gongalongs turned somersaults on the tightrope. The moon hung in the night sky, shining its light on the waves.

'Do you think,' said Betsy, 'if I gave Layla Rose my golden seahorse necklace it might cheer her up?'

'You mean, give it away as in give it away for good?' asked Mr Tiger.

'Yes,' said Betsy. 'For good.'

Mr Tiger took out his pocket-watch and studied it for a while.

'I suggest that you put it in the teapot and put the teapot in the sea.'

Betsy dropped the golden seahorse down the spout. She took off her silver shoes, tucked up her dress and, careful not to get it wet, she paddled into the water and watched the gentle tide take the teapot away.

'I do hope it won't lose its lid again,' said Betsy.

As they watched, the teapot disappeared beneath the waves.

They had just reached the steps that led up to the garden when Betsy heard her name being called. She glanced round but could see no one. Then she heard it again. She turned and looked out to sea and there in the moonlight were a mermaid and a merman, waving to her.

'Thank you,' called Layla Rose. 'You broke the spell.'

'With all our hearts, we thank you,' called the mer-prince.

And they swam away together into their happy-ever-after.

'Crumble cakes,' said Betsy. 'Why did it work this time and not the first time?'

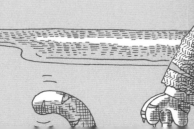

'Because this time you gave your golden seahorse to Layla Rose and you didn't expect it back,' said Mr Tiger. 'It was a true gift and that was the magic.'

'You know,' said Betsy, taking Mr Tiger's paw, 'I've had the best of adventures with you — on land, high in the sky and under the sea. You will always come back to the island left off the map of the world, won't you?'

'As long as you believe in magic, Betsy K Glory, I will always be there,' said Mr Tiger.

'And now, shall we see how high
we can jump together?'

195

AUTHOR'S NOTE

The alphabet is one of the unsung heroes of literature. Its elasticity has given us a paint pot of words and all that is required of you is a love of language and the imagination to use it spectacularly.

A huge thank you to Nick Maland whose amazing drawings have been the making of this series, bringing a special charm and originality to my stories. A big shout out to my fabulous editor Fiona Kennedy — it's been a pleasure as always to work with her. I'm very grateful to

my starry agent Catherine Clarke
who looks after me, and to Jacky
Bateman who manages to keep me on
the right path. My thanks to Jade
for handling publicity and Alex for
negotiating foreign rights, to Jessie
and Clémence for their design and
production care, and to all those in
the sales team who work so hard to
get my books into the shops.

Lastly, Mr Tiger would like to thank
Mr Joseph Salim Peress for inventing
the diving suit that gave him the idea
of designing one for himself.

Sally Gardner
Hastings
November 2019

You can also enjoy

MR TIGER, BETSY
and the **BLUE MOON**

&

MR TIGER, BETSY
and the **SEA DRAGON**

Out now in paperback!

MR TIGER, BETSY
and the
BLUE MOON

Read the first book in Sally Gardner's enchanting new series, illustrated by Nick Maland.

When Betsy K Glory, the daughter of a mermaid and an ice cream maker, meets the mysterious Mr Tiger they have a giant challenge ... a moon to turn blue, berries to collect and wishable-delicious ice cream to create. The sort that makes wishes come true.

Out now in paperback!

MR TIGER, BETSY
and the
SEA DRAGON

A red rogue wind blows a wicked pirate
captain close to the island left off the
map of the world. He's searching for
solid gold apples from the sea dragon's
orchard beneath the waves.

Betsy K Glory and Mr Tiger take to the
air and dive deep to save all the sea
dragon's treasures, including a
very precious egg.

At Zephyr we are proud to publish books you can read and re-read time and time again because they tell a brilliant story and because they entertain you.

Subscribe to our newsletter to hear all the latest news about upcoming releases, competitions and to have the chance to win signed books. Just drop us a line at hello@headofzeus.com